6
six
●●●●●●

7
seven
●●●●●●●

8
eight
●●●●●●●●

9
nine
●●●●●●●●●

10
ten
●●●●●●●●●●

16
sixteen
●●●●●●●●●●
●●●●●●

17
seventeen
●●●●●●●●●●
●●●●●●●

18
eighteen
●●●●●●●●●●
●●●●●●●●

19
nineteen
●●●●●●●●●●
●●●●●●●●●

20
twenty
●●●●●●●●●●
●●●●●●●●●●

26
twenty-six
●●●●●●●●●●
●●●●●●●●●●
●●●●●●○

27
twenty-seven
●●●●●●●●●●
●●●●●●●●●●
●●●●●●●

28
twenty-eight
●●●●●●●●●●
●●●●●●●●●●
●●●●●●●●

29
twenty-nine
●●●●●●●●●●
●●●●●●●●●●
●●●●●●●●●

30
thirty
●●●●●●●●●●
●●●●●●●●●●
●●●●●●●●●●○

36
thirty-six
●●●●●●●●●●
●●●●●●●●●●
●●●●●●●●●●
●●●●●●○

37
thirty-seven
●●●●●●●●●●
●●●●●●●●●●
●●●●●●●●●●
●●●●●●●○

38
thirty-eight
●●●●●●●●●●
●●●●●●●●●●
●●●●●●●●●●
●●●●●●●●

39
thirty-nine
●●●●●●●●●●
●●●●●●●●●●
●●●●●●●●●●
●●●●●●●●●

40
forty
●●●●●●●●●●
●●●●●●●●●●
●●●●●●●●●●
●●●●●●●●●●

46
forty-six
●●●●●●●●●●
●●●●●●●●●●
●●●●●●●●●●
●●●●●●●●●●
●●●●●●○

47
forty-seven
●●●●●●●●●●
●●●●●●●●●●
●●●●●●●●●●
●●●●●●●●●●
●●●●●●●○

48
forty-eight
●●●●●●●●●●
●●●●●●●●●●
●●●●●●●●●●
●●●●●●●●●●
●●●●●●●●○

49
forty-nine
●●●●●●●●●●
●●●●●●●●●●
●●●●●●●●●●
●●●●●●●●●●
●●●●●●●●●

50
fifty
●●●●●●●●●●
●●●●●●●●●●
●●●●●●●●●●
●●●●●●●●●●
●●●●●●●●●●

DISNEY

My First

1 2 3's

Disney PRESS

New York
An Imprint of Disney Book Group

Written by Thea Feldman
Educational consultant: Darlene Freeman

Printed in the United States of America
First Edition
Library of Congress Cataloging-in-Publication Data on file
ISBN-13: 978-1-4231-0225-0
ISBN-10: 1-4231-0225-8

For more Disney fun, visit www.disneybooks.com

Parent's Page

As an award-winning early-childhood educator for over twenty-five years, I am pleased to have had the opportunity to collaborate on the development of *Disney My First 1,2,3s*—a book that makes numbers come alive through the entertaining antics of many of your child's favorite Disney characters. The familiarity of these characters will immediately engage your child in the math activities that follow. Visual representations, creatively crafted exploratory questions, and hands-on materials have been specially designed to clarify your child's understanding of numbers, and to provide your child with a solid, meaningful foundation for learning more advanced concepts in the future.

Your child will learn:
- To recognize the role numbers play in our day-to-day lives
- To count from 1–100, by 1s, 2s, 5s, and 10s
- To see patterns as a special way of grouping numbers—for counting purposes
- To identify the meaning of numbers through the process of one-to-one correspondence
- To associate a number "word" with the actual number of items in a group
- To visualize and apply the concept of "one more"
- To compare quantities
- To work with the number concepts that form the basis of addition
- To visually conceptualize the base-ten number system

How to use this book with your child:
- At the start of each page, ask your child to describe what is happening.
- Draw your child's attention to the way the objects or characters on each page are arranged and grouped.
- Ask your child to identify how many objects are in each group.
- Ask your child to describe the pattern in the counting diagram at the top of each page. When you go on to the next page, ask your child how the diagram has changed.
- Assist your child with any activities that require the use of coins or manipulatives.

—Darlene Freeman

Table of Contents

Home and

Family

Get ready to count your favorite friends

and their families. Let's meet 1  and

his 2 . See what it's like to have

6 . And let's do some superhero

work and help 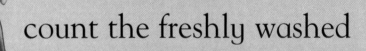 count the freshly washed

! needs a lot of help to count

all his dad's. But do you want to tell

that he has to try on 14?

Simba is Born!

- Can you find one (1) new baby at Pride Rock?

- Can you find and count his two (2) proud parents?

- Put a yellow card on each lion. How many lions are there in total?

two

BONUS BOX

A pair is two (2) things that belong together, such as two (2) shoes, two (2) eyes, two (2) wings—or two (2) animals, like Mufasa and Sarabi.
- Can you find five (5) other pairs of animals?
- Put one (1) orange card on each pair you find.

Donald's on the Ball!

Donald loves to coach his three (3) nephews when they play soccer.

Point to each nephew—Huey, Dewey, and Louie.

- Then put one (1) yellow card on each nephew and one (1) orange card on Donald.

- How many ducks are there in this family? Count them.

BONUS BOX

- Put an orange card on the duck that is closest to the ball.
- Put a red card on the duck that is the farthest from the ball.

Ariel Sings a Solo

- Put a yellow card on each of Ariel's sisters.

- Count as you put each card down.

- Can you find all six (6) of Ariel's sisters?

six

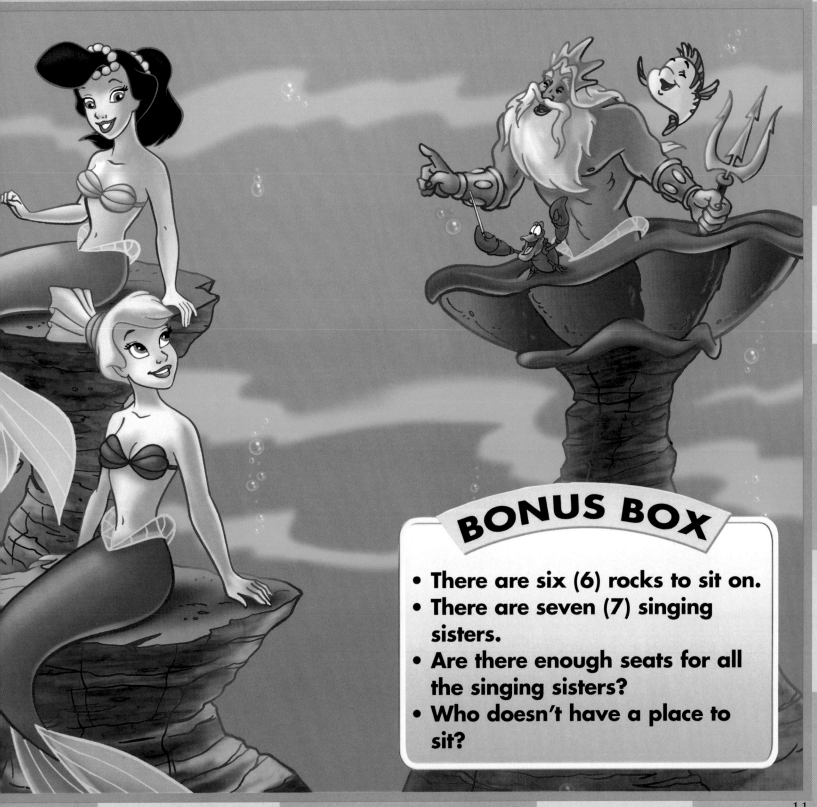

BONUS BOX

- There are six (6) rocks to sit on.
- There are seven (7) singing sisters.
- Are there enough seats for all the singing sisters?
- Who doesn't have a place to sit?

Snow White Says, "Welcome Home"

- Put one (1) yellow card on each Dwarf. Then count the Dwarfs.
- Can you name each one?
- Put an orange card on Snow White.
- How many yellow cards and orange cards are there altogether?
- Line up all the cards and count them.

8

eight

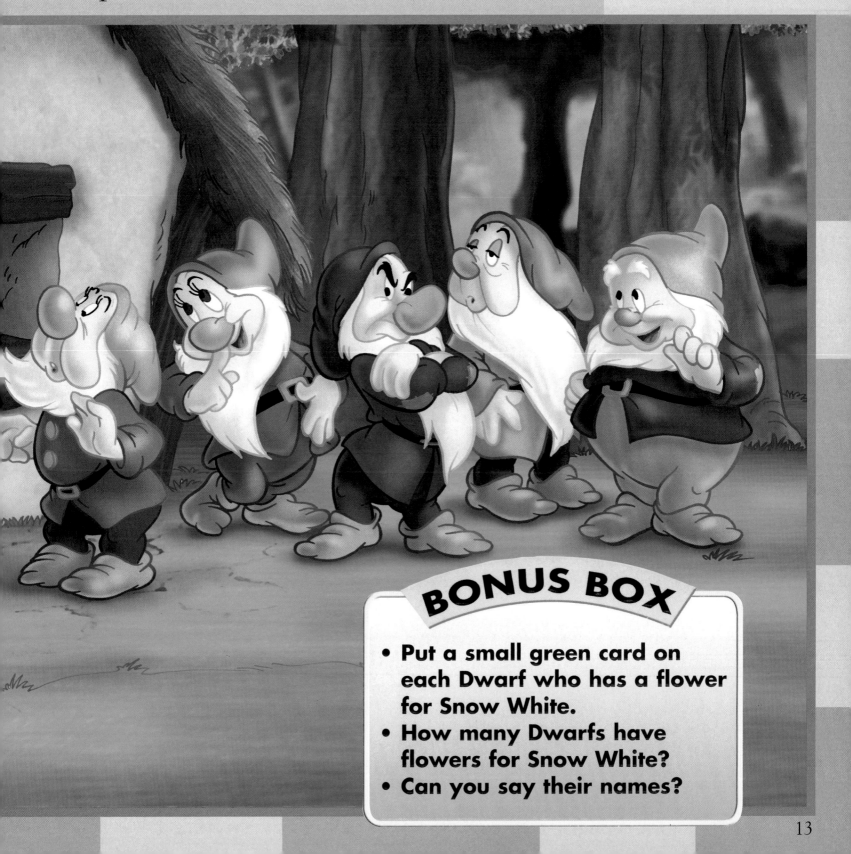

BONUS BOX

- Put a small green card on each Dwarf who has a flower for Snow White.
- How many Dwarfs have flowers for Snow White?
- Can you say their names?

It's Laundry Day at

The Parrs do a lot of normal, everyday things, like laundry.

- Put a red card on each freshly washed red shirt.
- How many red shirts are hanging on the line?

14

the Parrs

- Put a green card on the freshly washed blue shirt.
- How many shirts are hanging on the line altogether?
- Count them to find out.

ten

BONUS BOX

Which is more, nine (9) shirts or one (1) shirt?

Cinderella Leaves the Ball

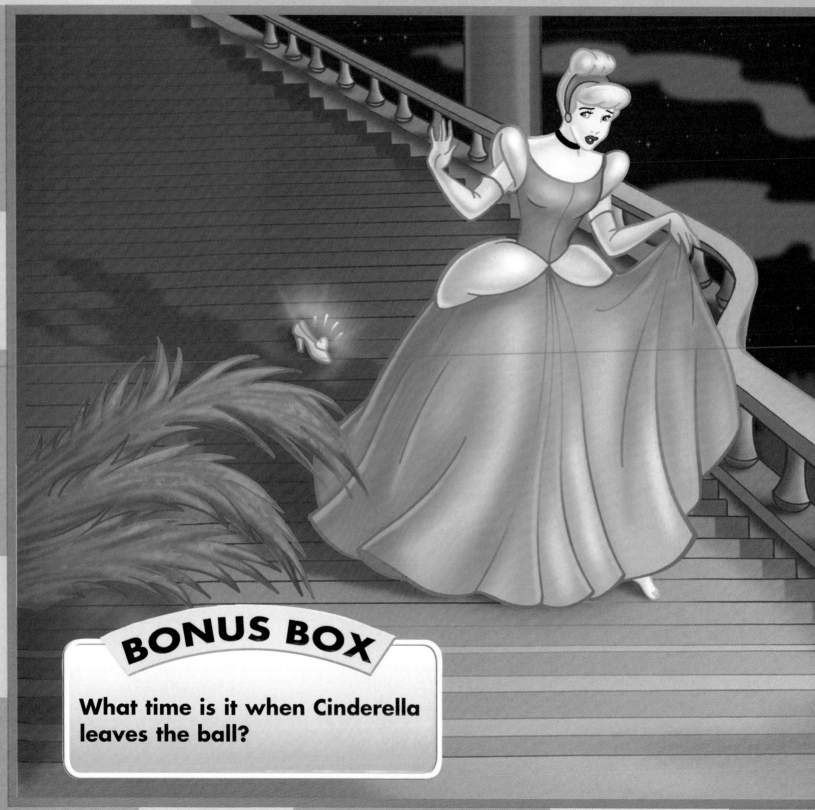

BONUS BOX

What time is it when Cinderella leaves the ball?

Put green number cards on the clock so
Cinderella will know what time it is.
Start at one (1) and end with twelve (12).

twelve

13

thirteen

Lilo Shares Her Muumuus

- Put a yellow card on the muumuu Stitch is trying on.

- Put red cards on thirteen (13) other muumuus.

- How many muumuus are there altogether?

14

fourteen

BONUS BOX

How many muumuus are red?

Nemo's Off to School!

- Nemo thought there were fifteen (15) anemone homes near his home.

- Then he discovered one (1) more.

- That makes sixteen (16) anemone homes in Nemo's neighborhood.

- Put a red card on each one.

16

sixteen

BONUS BOX

- Put one (1) yellow card on each anemone that is bright yellow.
- Count them.
- How many are there?

Chicken Little's Trophies

BUCK'S TROPHIES

- Chicken Little thought he counted seventeen (17) trophies in his father's trophy case. But when he looked more closely, it seemed like his father had eighteen (18) trophies.

- Put a green card on each trophy.

- Then line up all the cards and count them.

- Did Chicken Little's father have seventeen (17) or eighteen (18) trophies?

18

eighteen

BONUS BOX

- **How many trophies does Chicken Little have?**
- **Who has more trophies, Chicken Little or his dad?**

19

nineteen

The Beast's Kitchen

It's time for spring cleaning, and all the dishes in the Beast's castle are being washed.

- There are twenty (20) dinner plates that need to be washed.
- Nineteen (19) of the dinner plates are round, and one (1) dinner plate is a rectangle.

- Place a coin on each round dinner plate, and a yellow rectangular card on the rectangular dinner plate.
- Then count each coin and card as you remove it from the picture.
- How many coins and cards are there?
- How many dinner plates are there?

20

twenty

BONUS BOX

- Name the shapes of the dinner plates.
- How many different shapes are there?

Find the Pairs!

- How good is your memory?
- Cover each picture with one (1) red card.

- Then pick up two (2) cards, one (1) at a time, to try to find matching pairs of pictures.
- If it's a match, keep the cards.
- If it's not a match, put the cards back.
- Keep going until you have collected all the cards.

A Review for You!

1
one
●

2
two
● ●

5
five
● ● ● ● ●

6
six
● ● ● ● ● ●

9
nine
● ● ● ● ● ● ● ● ●

10
ten
● ● ● ● ● ● ● ● ● ●

13
thirteen
● ● ● ● ● ● ● ● ● ●
● ● ●

14
fourteen
● ● ● ● ● ● ● ● ● ●
● ● ● ●

17
seventeen
● ● ● ● ● ● ● ● ● ●
● ● ● ● ● ● ●

18
eighteen
● ● ● ● ● ● ● ● ● ●
● ● ● ● ● ● ● ●

28

Each of these numbers is now your new friend.
Count them out loud from beginning to end.

three

four

seven

eight

eleven

twelve

fifteen

sixteen

nineteen

twenty

Town and

Country

There's so much to count in the great outdoors! How many [trees] do [Beast] and [Belle] stroll past? Can you count all the [snowballs] that [Mike] tosses at [Sulley]? And there are so many different kinds of animals, too! Let's count [dogs], [turtles], [rabbits], and even some [camels]!

Lady and Tramp in the Park

Lady and Tramp see all their doggy friends every day.

- Today there are twenty-two (22) dogs in the park, including Lady and Tramp.
- Can you count by ones (1s) or twos (2s) to count them all?

22

twenty-two

BONUS BOX

- Lady and Tramp are a pair of dogs that don't look alike.
- Some pairs of dogs do look alike. Put a yellow card on each pair you find.
- How many pairs of dogs can you find?

Baloo and Mowgli Have Fun in the Jungle

Baloo shows Mowgli how to have a swinging good time in the jungle—swinging on vines, that is!

- Can you count twenty-three (23) vines hanging from the trees?

- Put a small green card on each one (1) as you count.

24

twenty-four

BONUS BOX

Find and point to the longest vine.

35

Sulley and Mike's Snowy Day

- Sulley built a snow fort to protect himself from the snowballs Mike was throwing at him.

- Sulley made twenty-five (25) snowballs to build his fort.

- How many are in each row? Count by ones (1s) or fives (5s) to count all the snowballs in Sulley's fort.

26

twenty-six

Pocahontas Looks for Leaves

Look! Thumper has some new cousins! Bambi and Flower came to meet them!

- Put a small green card on each bunny.

- Count each bunny as you put down the card.

- See if you can find all thirty-six (36) of Thumper's new bunny cousins.

36

thirty-six

BONUS BOX

- How many groups of three (3) bunnies do you see?
- Put one (1) yellow card on each group of three (3) bunnies.

Nemo and Marlin Ride the Waves!

The Eastern Australian Current is one fast place, dude! Marlin and Nemo ride the waves with thirty-seven (37) sea turtles. Find and count them all.

BONUS BOX

Can you find these three (3) groups?
1. The biggest turtles
2. The smallest turtles
3. The medium-size turtles

Busy, Busy Ants

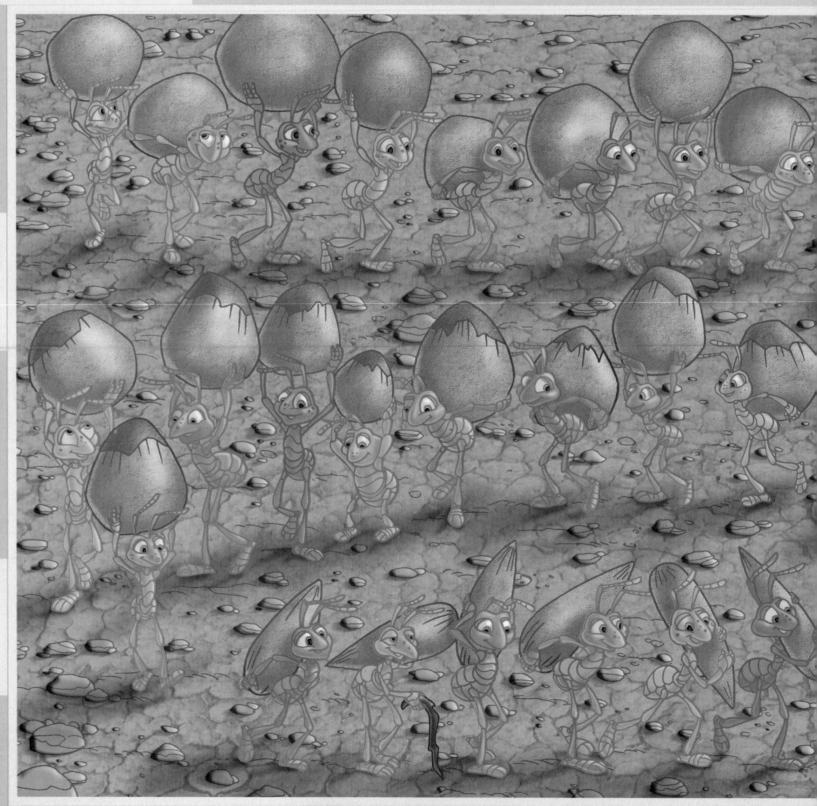

It's harvest time and the ants are busy carrying ripe grains. There are forty (40) ants. Each ant is carrying one (1) grain.

• How many grains are there?
• Count each grain to prove you are right.

40

forty

BONUS BOX

Can you find the ant who is carrying a grain that is a different color from the rest?

Four in a Row Tic-Tac-Toe!

Number of Players: One (1) or two (2)

Goal: To get four (4) in a row—horizontally, vertically, or diagonally

You will need:

• Thirty-two (32) small coins

• Number cards 21–40 placed in a small bag

FREE	32	22	34
36	25	28	27
26	29	31	30
21	33	23	FREE

How to Play:

1. Place a small coin on each square marked FREE.
2. Take turns pulling out a number card.
3. Say the number.
4. If either player has that number, cover the space with a coin.
5. The first person to cover four (4) numbers in a row is the winner.

FREE	27	30	39
28	31	38	33
40	35	24	37
32	29	34	FREE

A Review for You!

21
twenty-one

22
twenty-two

26
twenty-six

27
twenty-seven

28
twenty-eight

31
thirty-one

32
thirty-two

36
thirty-six

37
thirty-seven

38
thirty-eight

Each of these numbers is now your new friend.
Count them out loud from beginning to end.

23
twenty-three

24
twenty-four

25
twenty-five

29
twenty-nine

30
thirty

33
thirty-three

34
thirty-four

35
thirty-five

39
thirty-nine

40
forty

All Around

the Town

There are so many things to count all around the town! The bookshop is filled with [books] . The tire shop is well stocked with [tires] . The fruit seller has lots of [fruit] . You can help count [doors] at the scare factory. [workers] are counting on [Mr. Incredible] to save them. Find out how many [people] he saves when he stops the [train] !

Belle Gets Something to Read

BOOKSELLER

Belle ordered forty-two (42) books, and they just arrived. She needs the Beast's help to carry them.

- The Beast can put forty (40) books on his wagon.

- Belle will have to carry two (2).

- Can you count all forty-two (42) books?

42

forty-two

BONUS BOX

- **How many blue books do you see on the Beast's wagon?**
- **How many red ones?**
- **How many green ones?**
- **How many yellow ones?**

Luigi's Towers of Tires

11 TIRES

11 TIRES

11 TIRES

Luigi's Casa Della Tires is the place to go when you need new wheels!

- How many tires does Luigi have in his store?
- Count them to find out.

11 TIRES

BONUS BOX

Can you name three (3) different ways each pile of tires is the same?

Lady and Tramp's Dinner for Two!

Lady and Tramp come to Tony's for a romantic dinner. Tony is getting ready to put a red-and-white checked tablecloth on the table.

- Count the white squares on the tablecloth.
- Then count the red squares on the tablecloth.
- How many squares do you think there are altogether?
- Count them to find out.

BONUS BOX

- How many squares are in each row?
- How many rows are there?

Minnie's Mail

Minnie is having a big party. She is sending invitations to forty-eight (48) guests.

• Count the envelopes to make sure she has an invitation for each guest.

48

forty-eight

BONUS BOX

How many stamps are on Goofy's face?

Buzz on Main Street

Orange cones are a great way to stop traffic—if you're a toy!

Count all fifty (50) cones—those moving and those not!

50
fifty

BONUS BOX

- How many cones are moving?
- Place a green card on each one.

Mr. Incredible to the Rescue!

Stopping runaway trains is all in a day's work for Mr. Incredible. People are amazed at what he can do. Can you count fifty-two (52) faces watching at the windows?

BONUS BOX

- **Point to the first window of the train.**
- **Point to the last window.**
- **Which one has more faces behind it?**

Lilo and Stitch's Surfboard Search

Lilo is getting her very first surfboard! Stitch is getting one, too! Look at all the surfboards.

- Point to each one as you count the fifty-four (54) surfboards.
- Then point to the two (2) surfboards you think Lilo and Stitch might like best.

BONUS BOX

How many surfboards are in each group?

Sulley's on the Job

It's another busy day at the scare factory!

• Can you help Sulley count all fifty-six (56) doors he has to go through on his shift?

• Point to each one as you count it.

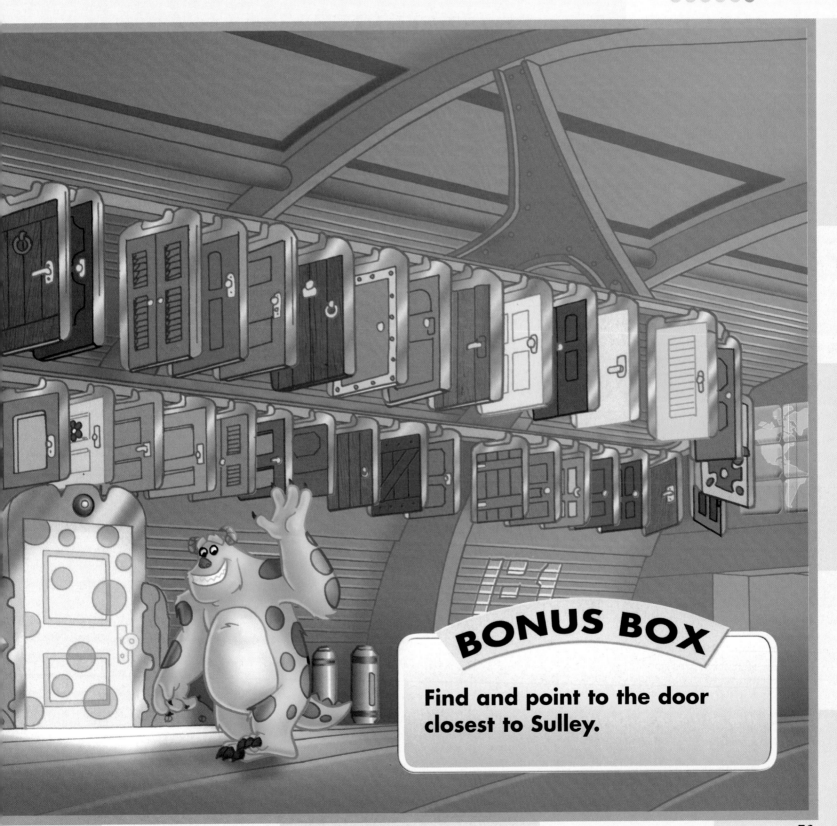

BONUS BOX

Find and point to the door closest to Sulley.

Abu and the Oranges

Abu loves fresh oranges! But the fruit seller doesn't like Abu! The fruit seller had fifty-eight (58) oranges, but Abu took one.

- How many are left?
- Count them to find out.

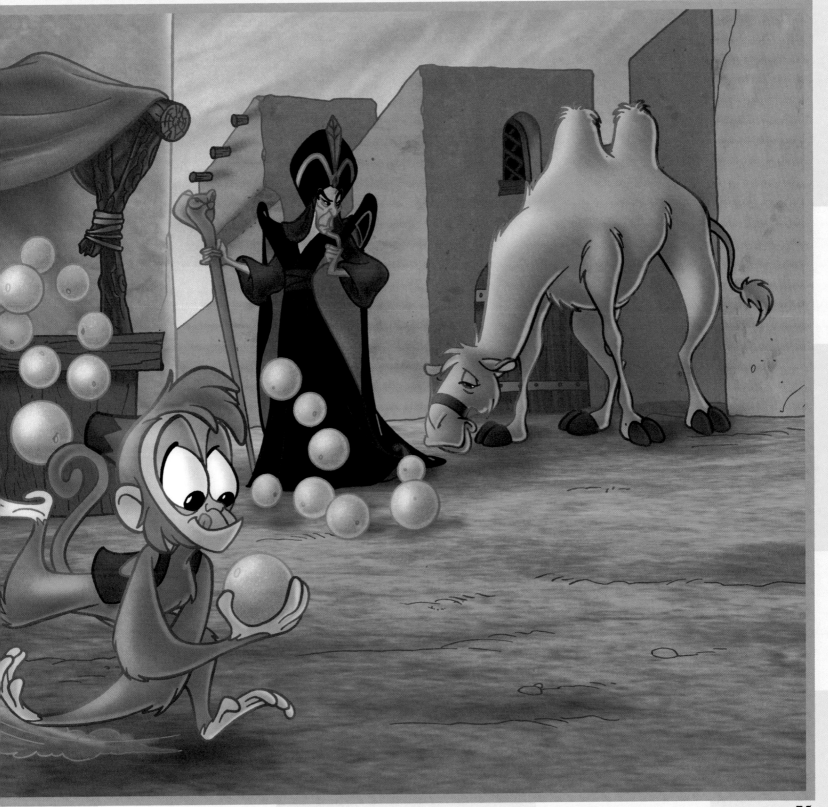

Tinker Bell's Got Work to Do!

All the fairies bring their pots and pans to Tink to be repaired.

- How many pots and pans need to be repaired?

- Count them by ones (1s) or tens (10s).

BONUS BOX

- There are six (6) groups of pots.
- Each group has ten (10) pots.
- Place an orange card on each group.

77

Help Chicken Little Find the Numbers

For this activity you will need:
20 small coins

Put a small coin on each of the following numbers you see in the picture.

(41) (42) (43) (44) (45) (46) (47) (48) (49) (50)

(51) (52) (53) (54) (55) (56) (57) (58) (59) (60)

A Review for You!

41

forty-one

42

forty-two

46

forty-six

47

forty-seven

48

forty-eight

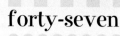

51

fifty-one

52

fifty-two

56

fifty-six

57

fifty-seven

58

fifty-eight

Each of these numbers is now your new friend.
Count them out loud from beginning to end.

43
forty-three

44
forty-four

45
forty-five

49
forty-nine

50
fifty

53
fifty-three

54
fifty-four

55
fifty-five

59
fifty-nine

60
sixty

Having Fun!

Everyone is spotted having fun sometimes!

Some 🐱🐱 just have to dance! So does

🧍‍♀️. Count all the 🕯️ that light up the 🤴's

ballroom! Have some 🍕 with 👧 and 👾

or 🍦 with 🐭🐭. Can you count the ways

you like to have fun?

61

The Aristocats Move to the Music

When Scat Cat and his band start to play, feet just start moving to the music!

- How many cats are on the dance floor?

- Count by ones (1s) or twos (2s) to find out.

62

sixty-two

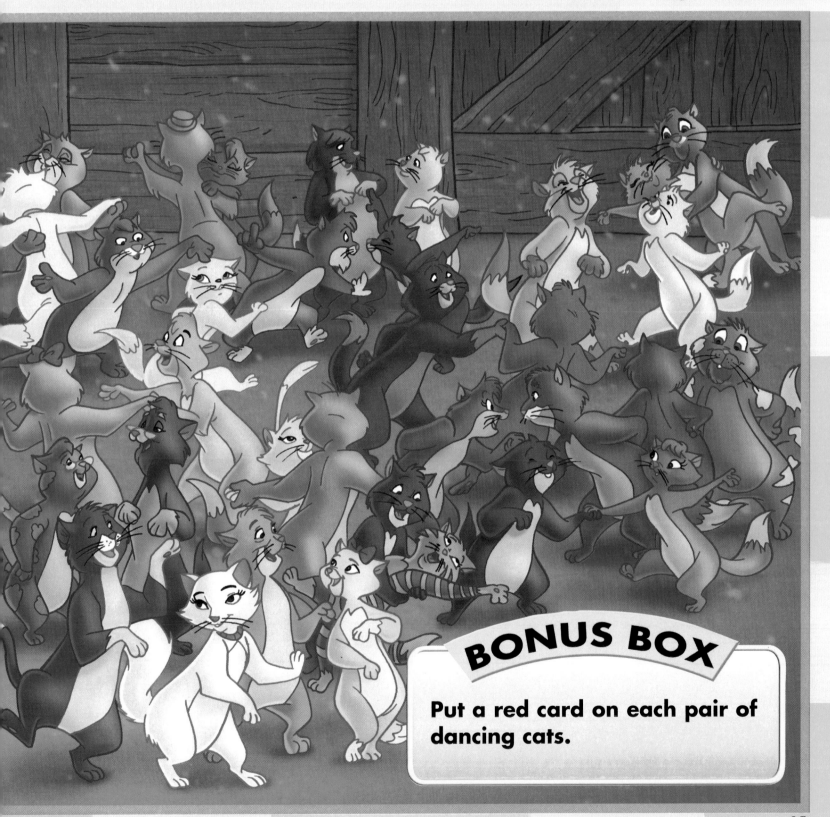

BONUS BOX

Put a red card on each pair of dancing cats.

Happy Birthday, Andy!

It's Andy's birthday and he's gotten sixty-four (64) presents! Wow! Can you count all the wrapped boxes?

sixty-four

BONUS BOX

Can you find four (4) differently shaped presents? Point to one (1) in the shape of a circle (●), one (1) in the shape of a rectangle (▬), one (1) in the shape of a square (■), and one (1) in the shape of a triangle (▲).

Ariel's Favorite Things

BONUS BOX

Can you spot all the things you could play with?

Ariel loves her treasures from the human world. Count all sixty-five (65) treasures by ones (1s) or fives (5s).

Sleeping Beauty's Forest Song

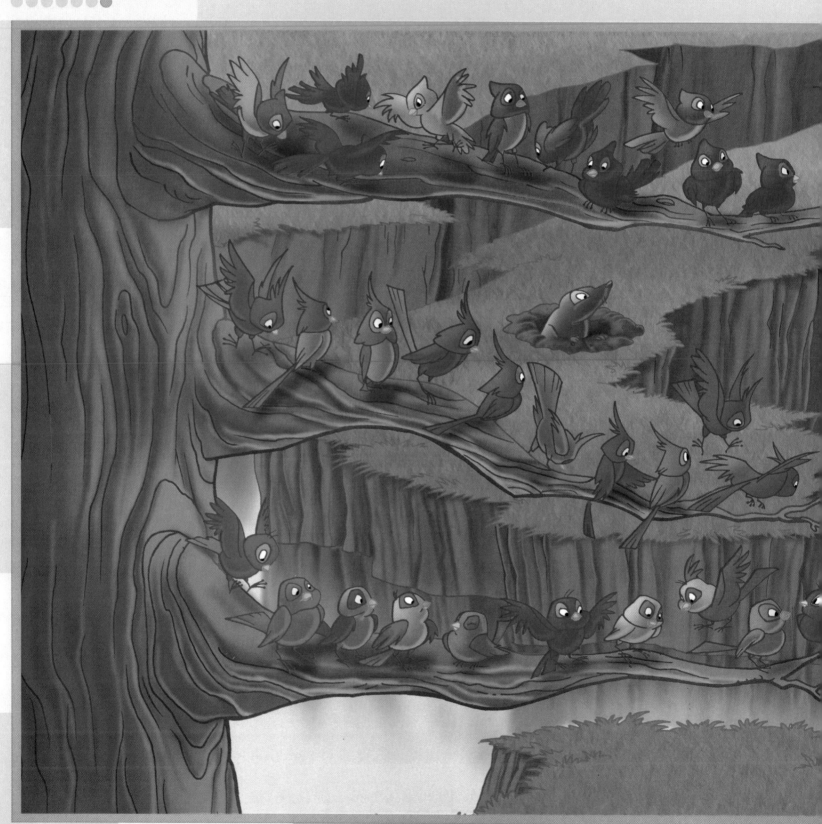

Sleeping Beauty sings so beautifully, all the birds of the forest come to listen.

- Ten (10) birds are sitting on each tree branch.

- Seven (7) birds are perched on Sleeping Beauty.

- Can you count sixty-seven (67) birds?

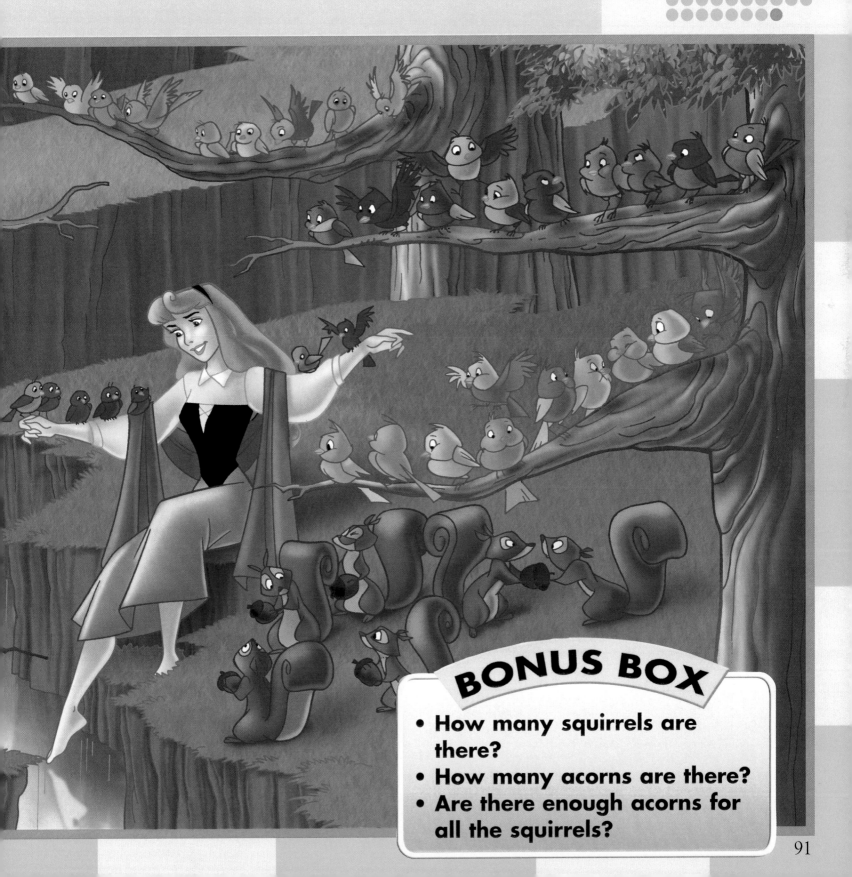

BONUS BOX

- How many squirrels are there?
- How many acorns are there?
- Are there enough acorns for all the squirrels?

Belle and the Beast Toast Marshmallows

Belle shows the Beast how to toast marshmallows. Yum! He's ready to eat a Beast-size share of them!

- How many marshmallows are on each stick?
- How many marshmallows are on each plate?
- Can you count all seventy (70) marshmallows by ones (1s) or tens (10s)?

70

seventy

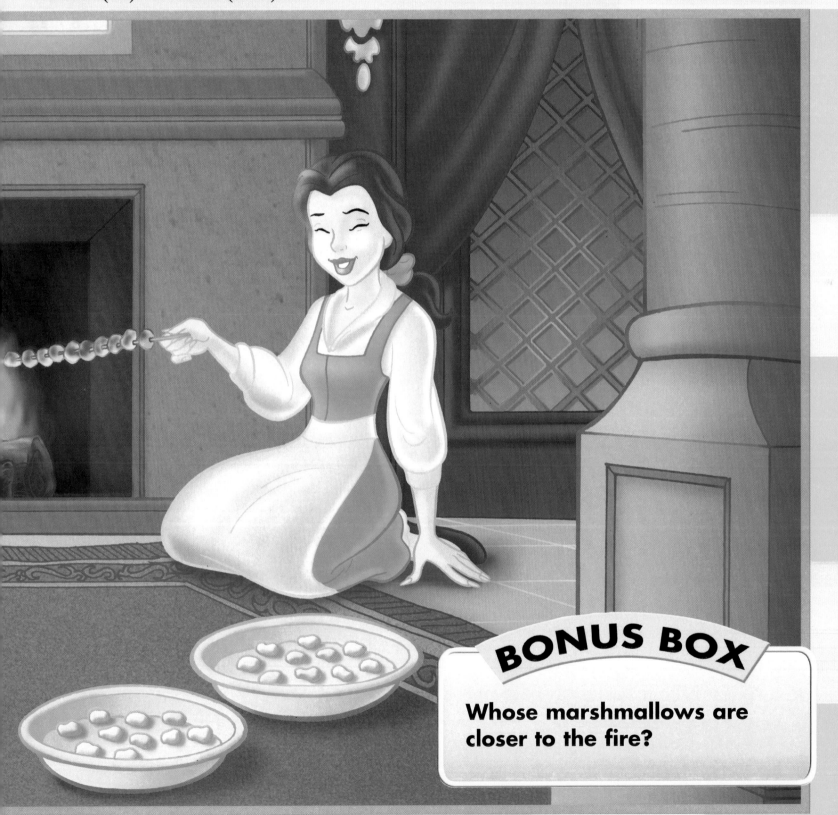

BONUS BOX

Whose marshmallows are closer to the fire?

Chicken Little's Up at Bat

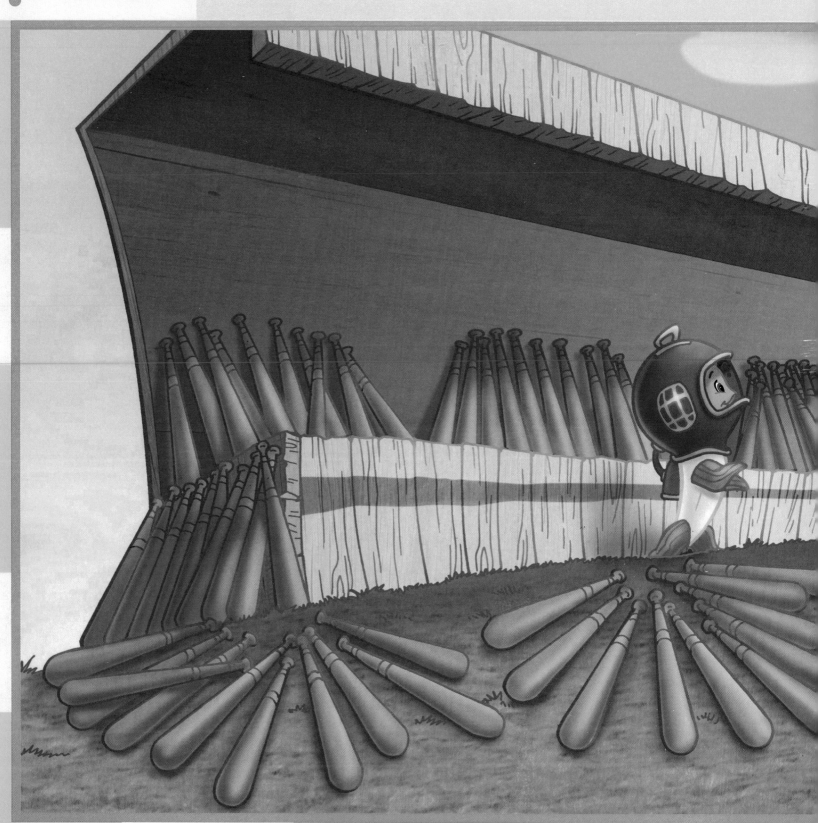

The Oakey Oaks baseball team has seventy-two (72) bats.
And before he got his game winning hit,
Chicken Little struck out with them all!
Can you count all seventy-two (72) bats?

72

seventy-two

BONUS BOX

Chicken Little just hit the ball. It's headed toward the outfield. Point in the direction the ball is going.

A Goofy Ice-Cream Contest

Nothing is more fun than an ice-cream-eating contest. How many scoops does each contestant need to eat? How many scoops is the referee eating? Can you count all seventy-three (73) scoops—quick, before they melt!

BONUS BOX

Who has more scoops to eat, Mickey or the referee?

Balloons for Boo

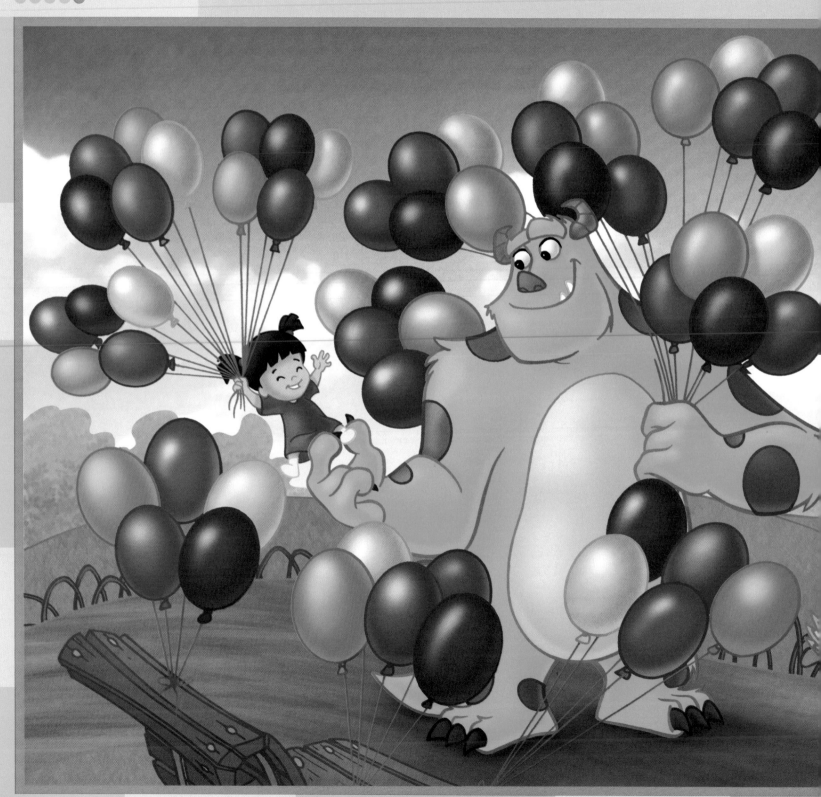

Sulley knows that Boo really likes balloons, so he bought all of them for her.

- There are seventy-five (75) altogether.
- Can you count all of them by ones (1s) or fives (5s)?
- Place a red card on each group of five (5) balloons.

BONUS BOX

Put down a coin for each color balloon you see. Start with one (1) coin for red. How many different colors are there?

Pizza Party
for Two

Lilo and Stitch ordered pizza for dinner—a lot of pizza. Stitch has already tasted seventy-six (76) slices, and has two (2) more to go.

• Count all seventy-eight (78) slices of pizza.

seventy-eight

BONUS BOX

How many slices are there in each whole pizza? How many whole pizzas are there?

79

Cinderella and the Prince in the Ballroom

It's magical when Cinderella and the Prince dance in the candlelit ballroom.

• Can you count eighty (80) glowing candles in the candelabras and on the tables?

eighty

BONUS BOX

• How many candles are on each table?
• How many candles are in each candelabra?

You Can Count on Sulley Being Scary

For this activity you will need:
Ten (10) green cards and ten (10) red cards.

1. Put green cards on ten (10) numbers that appear on hats.

2. Put red cards on ten (10) numbers that appear on balloons.

BONUS BOX

1. What is the same about the numbers on the hats?
2. What is the same about the numbers on the balloons?

105

A Review for You!

61
sixty-one

62
sixty-two

66
sixty-six

67
sixty-seven

68
sixty-eight

71
seventy-one

72
seventy-two

76
seventy-six

77
seventy-seven

78
seventy-eight

Each of these numbers is now your new friend.
Count them out loud from beginning to end.

63
sixty-three

64
sixty-four

65
sixty-five

69
sixty-nine

70
seventy

73
seventy-three

74
seventy-four

75
seventy-five

79
seventy-nine

80
eighty

Numbers Are

Everywhere

You can count   with   under the sea. Or count   way up in the sky with   . How about counting things you've never seen before, like   with   , or   if you live in Oakey Oaks with   .

Whatever you do, wherever you go, it's fun to take time to do some counting!

Daisy Loves Daisies!

- How many daisies are in each row of Daisy's garden?

- How many rows of daisies are there? Count by ones (1s) or tens (10s) to find out how many daisies are in the garden. If you add the daisy in Donald's hand, there will be eighty-one (81) altogether.

BONUS BOX

- How many petals has Donald plucked from the flower?
- How many are left on the flower? How many petals are there altogether?

Mowgli and Baloo at the Man-Village

Mowgli can't believe how many huts are in the Man-Village!

• Help Mowgli count all eighty-four (84) huts.

BONUS BOX

- Put a yellow card on each group of huts.
- How many groups of huts are there?
- How many huts are in each group?

Ariel's Seashell Collection

- Ariel has eighty-five (85) seashells in her collection.

- She put them in groups of five (5).

- She loves to count them all.

- Why don't you count them with her? Count by ones (1s) or fives (5s).

- Place a red card on each group of five (5).

86

eighty-six

BONUS BOX

- Ariel's collection has many kinds of shells, but there is more of one kind than any of the others.

- Is it the ⬛ , ⬛ , ⬛ , ⬛ , or ⬛ ?

87

eighty-seven

The Aristocats' Music Lesson

- Sometimes it sounds like Scat Cat is hitting all eighty-eight (88) keys at once!
- Count all the piano keys with Scat Cat!
- Start with the black keys.
- Then go on to the white keys.

88

eighty-eight

BONUS BOX

- **How many black keys are there? Point to and count each one.**
- **Now count the white keys.**

Chicken Little Says Good-bye

Chicken Little's new friends are leaving. Even though they'll be back again for acorns next year, there's not a dry eye when it comes time for saying good-bye.

- Thirty (30) aliens are getting ready to leave.

- They each have three (3) eyes.

- Can you count all ninety (90) eyes?

90

ninety

BONUS BOX

How many aliens are in each group?

Bambi's Rain Shower

It's raining in Bambi's forest today.

- How many raindrops are in each row?

- Count by tens (10s) to find ninety (90) raindrops.

- Then add the extra one (1) dripping on Flower.

Flik's Idea Takes Flight

It takes ninety (90) ants to pull Flik's bird invention to its launching pad. That's a lot! Can you count all those ants? If you add Flik, Dot, Princess Atta, and the Queen, how many ants would that be altogether?

BONUS BOX

How many ants are pulling each rope?

Lightning McQueen Courts Sally

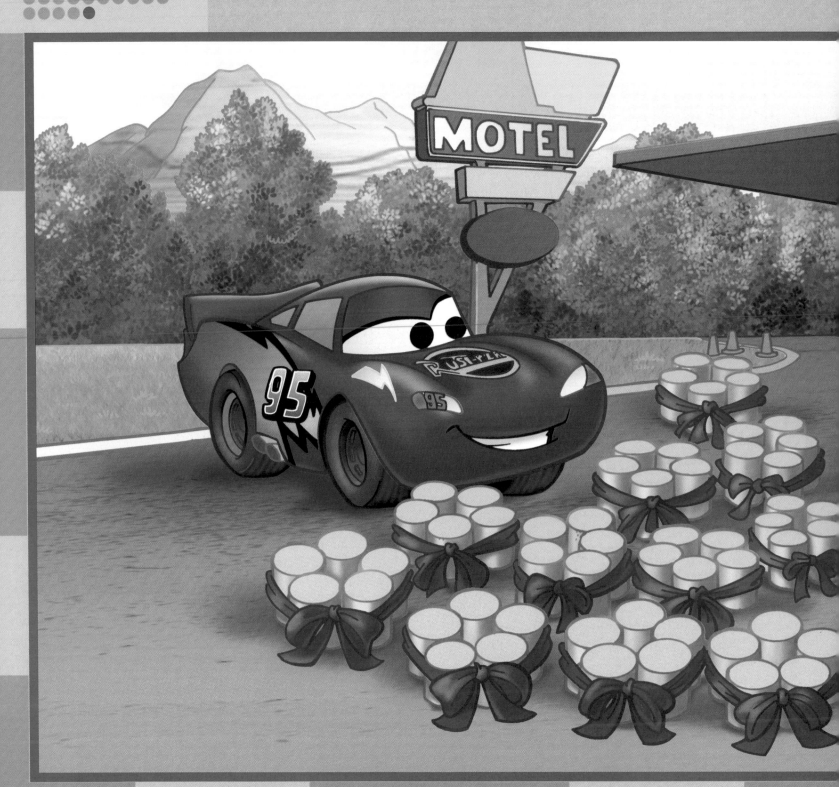

Lightning McQueen likes courting Sally.

- Lightning is giving Sally a gift of ninety-five (95) cans of motor oil.

- Can you count all ninety-five (95) cans?

- Try to count them by ones (1s) or fives (5s).

BONUS BOX

- Put a green card on each group of oil cans you see.
- How many cans are in each group?

The Fairies' Picnic

It's a beautiful day, so Tink and the other fairies decide to have a picnic. They go off in pairs.

• Put a green card on each pair.

• Then count by twos (2s) to find all ninety-eight (98) fairies.

BONUS BOX

Put one (1) red card on each pair of fairies that is eating. How many pairs of fairies are eating?

127

Simba and the Night Sky

- Simba looks up to count the twinkling stars in the night sky above the Pride Lands.

- Help Simba count one hundred (100) stars.

100
one hundred

BONUS BOX

Can you find the biggest and brightest star in the sky?

A Review for You!

 **81**
eighty-one

 **82**
eighty-two

 **86**
eighty-six

 **87**
eighty-seven

 **88**
eighty-eight

 **91**
ninety-one

92
ninety-two

 **96**
ninety-six

97
ninety-seven

 **98**
ninety-eight

Each of these numbers is now your new friend.
Count them out loud from beginning to end.

83 eighty-three

84 eighty-four

85 eighty-five

89 eighty-nine

90 ninety

93 ninety-three

94 ninety-four

95 ninety-five

99 ninety-nine

100 one hundred

100's a Crowd!

Put a card or a coin on each picture that shows a place where you might find one hundred (100) (or more) people. That's a lot!

At a Farm

At the Park

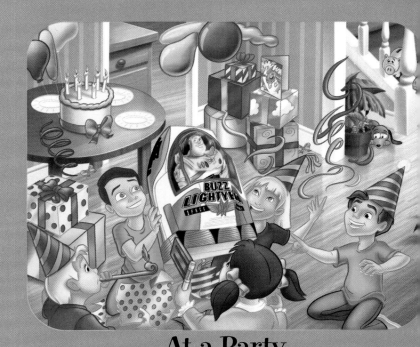

At a Party

At the Circus

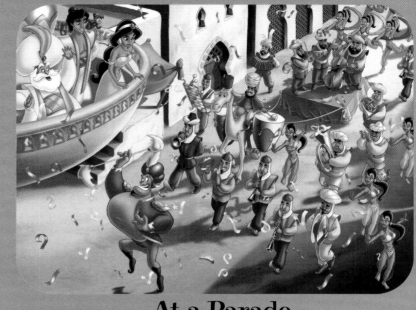

At a Parade

At a Fair

At a Pet Shop

Around Town

At the Movies

Counting to Ten

Place a large orange card on each picture that shows more than ten (10) characters. Place a small green card on each picture that shows fewer than ten (10) characters. Can you find the one (1) picture with exactly ten (10) characters?

How Many Dalmatians?

1 one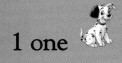

2 two

3 three

4 four

5 five

6 six

7 seven

8 eight

9 nine

10 ten

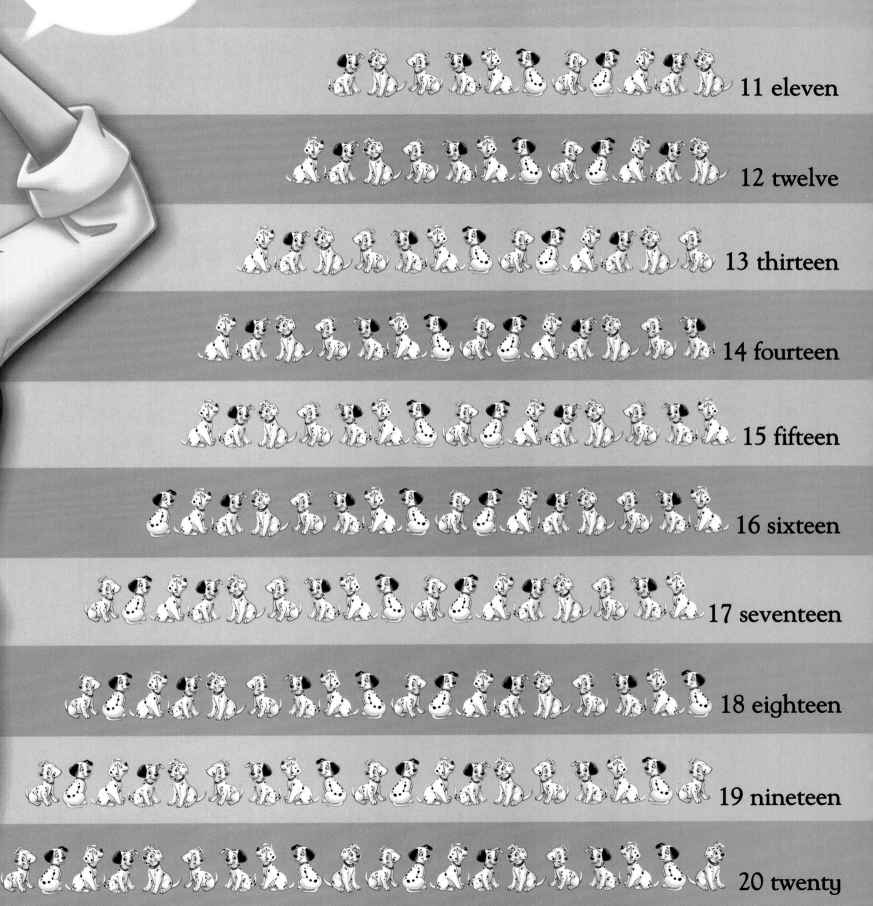

"How many puppies are there?"

11 eleven

12 twelve

13 thirteen

14 fourteen

15 fifteen

16 sixteen

17 seventeen

18 eighteen

19 nineteen

20 twenty

137

BONUS BOX ANSWER KEY

PAGE 7:

PAGE 9:

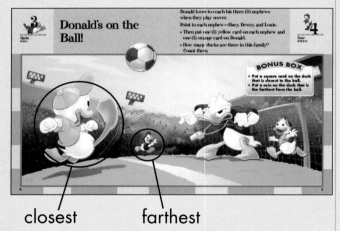

closest   farthest

PAGE 11:
Ariel doesn't have a place to sit.

PAGE 13:

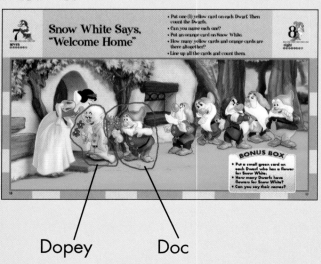

Dopey   Doc

PAGE 15:
Nine is more than one.

PAGE 16:
Midnight

PAGE 19:
Nine muumuus are red.

PAGE 21:
Ten anemones are bright yellow.

PAGE 23:
Chicken Little has no trophies. Buck has more trophies than Chicken Little.

PAGE 25:
The twenty dinner plates are nineteen circles and one rectangle. There are two different shapes.

PAGE 33:
There are six pairs of dogs that look alike. There are eleven pairs of dogs total.

PAGE 35:

PAGE 39:
There are more yellow leaves than orange leaves.

PAGE 41:

PAGE 43:
The gardener will plant a cherry tree next.

PAGE 45:
The birds make a *V* shape in the sky.

PAGE 47:
There are twelve groups of bunnies.

PAGE 49:

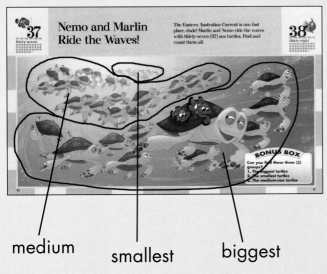

medium   smallest   biggest

PAGE 51:

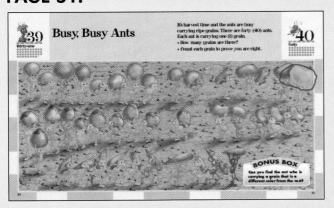

PAGE 59:
There are ten yellow, ten blue, ten red, and ten green books.

PAGE 61:
All the tires are black. There are eleven tires in each pile. All the tires are round. All the tires are the same size.

PAGE 63:
There are five squares in each row. There are nine rows.

PAGE 65:
There are four stamps on Goofy's face.

PAGE 67:

PAGE 69:
The last window has more faces behind it.

PAGE 71:
There are nine surfboards in each group.

PAGE 73:

PAGE 77:

PAGE 79:

PAGE 85:

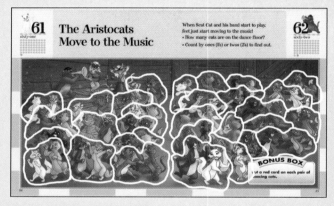

PAGE 87:

PAGE 88:

PAGE 91:

There are six squirrels. There are five acorns. There are not enough acorns for all the squirrels.

PAGE 93:

Belle's marshmallows are closer to the fire.

PAGE 97:

Mickey has more scoops of ice cream than the referee.

PAGE 99:

There are five colors — purple, red, blue, yellow, and green.

PAGE 101:

There are five slices in each whole pizza. There are fifteen whole pizzas.

PAGE 103:

There are ten candles on each table. There are ten candles in each candelabra.

PAGE 105:

The numbers on the hats are all in the sixties. The numbers on the balloons are all in the seventies.

PAGE 111:

Donald has plucked eight petals. There are two petals left on the flower. There are ten petals altogether.

PAGE 113:

There are twelve groups of huts. There are seven huts in each group.

PAGE 113:

There are more than any other shell.

PAGE 117:

There are thirty-six black keys. There are fifty-two white keys.

PAGE 119:

There are three aliens in each group.

PAGE 123:

There are fifteen ants pulling on each rope.

PAGE 125:

There are five oil cans in each group.

PAGE 127:

There are three pairs of fairies eating.

PAGE 129:

PAGE 132:

You might find one hundred or more people at the circus, at a parade, at a fair, and around town.

PAGE 134:

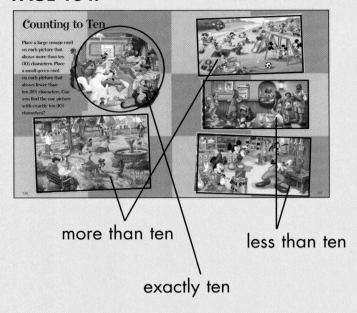

more than ten

less than ten

exactly ten

INDEX

83 84 85

96

86 87 88 89 90

97

91 92 93 94 95

98

99 100 101

 **51** fifty-one

 **52** fifty-two

 **53** fifty-three

 **54** fifty-four

 **55** fifty-five

 **61** sixty-one

 **62** sixty-two

 **63** sixty-three

 **64** sixty-four

 **65** sixty-five

 **71** seventy-one

 **72** seventy-two

 **73** seventy-three

 **74** seventy-four

 **75** seventy-five

 **81** eighty-one

 **82** eighty-two

 **83** eighty-three

 **84** eighty-four

 **85** eighty-five

 **91** ninety-one

 **92** ninety-two

 **93** ninety-three

 **94** ninety-four

 **95** ninety-five